beg.

Songs of Submission – Book One

CD Reiss

chapter one.

At the height of singing the last note, when my lungs were still full and I was switching from pure physical power to emotional thrust, I was blindsided by last night's dream. Like most dreams, it hadn't had a story. I was on top of a grand piano on the rooftop bar of Hotel K. The fact that the real hotel didn't have a piano on the roof notwithstanding, I was on it and naked from the waist down, propped on my elbows. My knees were spread further apart than physically possible. Customers drank their thirty-dollar drinks and watched as I sang. The song didn't have words, but I knew them well, and as the strange man with his head between my legs licked me, I sang harder and harder until I woke up with an arched back and soaked sheets, hanging on to a middle C for dear life.

Same as the last note of our last song, and I held it

like a stranger was pleasuring me on a nonexistent piano. I drew that last note out for everything it was worth, pulling from deep inside my diaphragm, feeling the song rattle the bones of my rib cage, sweat pouring down my face. It was my note. The dream told me so. Even after Harry stopped strumming and Gabby's keyboard softened to silence, I croaked out the last tearful strain as if gripping the edge of a precipice.

When I opened my eyes in the dark club, I knew I had them; every one of them stared at me as if I had just ripped out their souls, put them in envelopes, and sent them back to their mothers, COD. Even in the few silent seconds after I stopped, when most singers would worry that they'd lost the audience, I knew I hadn't; they just needed permission to applaud. When I smiled, permission was granted, and they clapped all right.

Our band, Spoken Not Stirred, had brought down the Thelonius Room. A year of writing and rehearsing the songs and a month getting bodies in the door had paid off right here, right now.

The crowd. That was what it was all about. That was why I busted my ass. That was why I had shut out everything in my life but putting a roof over my head and food in my mouth. I didn't want anything from them but that ovation.

I bowed and went off stage, followed by the band. Harry bolted to the bathroom to throw up, as always. I could still hear the applause and banging feet. The room held a hundred people, and the audience sounded like a thousand. I wanted to take the moment to bathe in something other than the disappointment and failure that accompanied a career in music, but I heard Gabrielle next to me, tapping her right thumb and middle finger. Her gaze was blank, settled in a corner, her eyes as big as teacups. I followed that gaze to exactly nothing. The corner was empty, but she stared as if a mirror into herself stood there, and she didn't like what she saw.

I glanced at Darren, our drummer. He stared back at me, then at his sister, who had tapped those fingers since puberty.

"Gabby," I said.

She didn't answer.

Darren poked her bicep. "Gabs? Shit together?"

"Fuck off, Darren," Gabby said flatly, not looking away from the empty corner.

Darren and I looked at each other. We were each other's first loves, back in L.A. Performing Arts High, and even after the soft, simple breakup, we had deepened our friendship to the point we didn't need to talk with words.

We said to each other, with our expressions, that Gabby was in trouble again.

"We rule!" Harry gave a fist pump as he exited the bathroom, still buttoning up his pants. "You were awesome." He punched me in the arm, oblivious to what was going on with Gabby. "My heart broke a little at 'Split Me.'"

"Thanks," I said without emotion. I did feel gratitude, but we had other concerns at the moment. "Where's Vinny?"

Our manager, Vinny Mardigian, appeared as if summoned, all glad-handing and smiles. Such a dick. I really couldn't stand him, but he'd seemed confident and competent when we met.

"You happy?" I said. "We sold all our tickets at full price. Now maybe next time we won't have to pay to play?"

"Hello, Monica Sexybitch." That was his pet name for me. The guy had the personality of a landfill and the drive of a shark in bloody waters. "Nice to see you too. I got Performer's Agency on the line. Their guy's right outside."

Great. I needed representation from the The Rinkydink Agency like I needed a hole in the head. But I was an artist, and I was supposed to take whatever the industry handed me with a smile and spread legs.

Vinny, of course, couldn't shut up worth a damn. He was high on Performer's Agency and the worldwide fame he thought they would get us. He didn't realize half a step forward was just as good as a full step back. "You got a crowd out there asking for an encore. Everybody here does their job, then everybody's happy."

I listened, and sure enough, they were still clapping, and Gabby was still staring into the corner.

chapter two.

Darren took Gabby home after the encore, which she played like the crazy prodigy she was, then she blanked out again. Her depression was ameliorated by music and brought on by just about anything, even if she was taking her meds.

She'd attempted suicide two years before after a few weeks of corner-staring and complaining of not being able to feel anything about anything. I'd been the one to find her in the kitchen, bleeding into the sink. That had been terrific for everyone. She took my second bedroom, and Darren moved from a roommate-infested guest house in West Hollywood to a studio a block away. We played music together because music was what we did, and because it kept Gabby sane, Darren close, and me from screwing up. But it didn't even keep us in hot dogs. We all worked, and until I got my current gig at the rooftop bar at Hotel K, I had to give up Starbucks because I couldn't rub two nickels together to make heat.

Because Spoken Not Stirred had drawn more people than the cost of our guaranteed tickets, we'd made three hundred dollars that night. Fifteen percent went to Vinny Landfillian. Sixty-eight dollars paid for Harry's parking ticket because he figured if he was loading his bass and amp, he could park in a loading zone on the Sunset Strip before six o'clock. We split the rest four ways.

Hotel K was a spanking new modernist, thirty-story diamond in a one-story stucco shitpile of a neighborhood. The rooftop bar thing in L.A. had gotten out of hand. You couldn't swing a dead talent agent without hitting some new construction with a barside pool on the roof and thumping music day and night. The upside of the epidemic was that waitress service was the norm, and tall, skinny girls who could slip between name-dropping drunks while holding heavy trays over their heads without clocking anyone were an absolute necessity. The downside for someone tall and skinny like myself was my replaceability. You couldn't swing a tall, skinny girl in L.A. without hitting another one.

Darren and I had taken too long discussing who would watch Gabby. He convinced her to stay at his place for the night, though "convinced" might not be the word to use when talking about someone who didn't care about where she slept, or anything, one way or the other.

I ran from the elevator to the hotel locker room, the fifty bucks I'd made for holding a hundred people in my palm light in my pocket. I peeled off my jacket and stuffed it in my locker, then pulled my shirt off. I didn't have a second to spare before Yvonne, who I was relieving, started chewing me out for stranding her on the floor. I yanked a low-cut dress that showed more leg than modesty out of my bag and wrestled into it.

"You're late," Freddie, my manager, said. He stank of cigarettes, which I found disgusting.

"I'm sorry, I had a gig." I kicked off my shoes and pulled my pants off from under my dress. I had no time to worry about what Freddie thought of me.

"Bully for you." Freddie crossed his arms, scrunching his brown pinstripe suit. He had a mole on his cheek and wore a puckered expression even when he looked down my shirt, which was almost every time we talked.

I didn't wait to argue. I slipped back into my shoes, slapped my locker shut, and ran toward the floor.

"Yvonne!" I caught her in the back hall as she folded a wad of tips into her pocket.

"Monica, girl! Where were you?"

"I'm sorry. Thanks for covering my tables. Can I make it up to you?"

"I don't get home in time, you can pay the sitter an extra hour."

"No problem," I said, though it was a big problem.

"Jonathan Drazen is at your table." She put her hand to her heart. "He's hot, and he'll tip if he likes what he sees. So be nice." She handed me the tickets for my station.

Drazen was my boss's boss. He owned the hotel. Apparently, he traveled a lot, and he spent little or no time on the roof when he was in town, so we hadn't met.

This development was more annoying than anything. I'd just gotten the ovation of my life at a really cool club and was bathing in the warm validation. I didn't need to prove myself all over again, and based on what? If it wasn't my music, I didn't care.

The place was packed: wall-to-wall Eurotrash, Hollywood heavyweights, and assorted hangers-on. The pool was a big rectangle in the center of the expanse. Red chairs surrounded it, and a large cocktail area with tables and chairs sat off to the side. Little tents with couches inside outlined most of the roof, and when the curtains closed, you left them closed unless someone looked as though they'd taken off without paying.

I stood at the service bar, flipping through my tickets. Five tables, two with little star punch-outs in the upper right hand corners. Put there by Freddie, they meant someone important was at the table. Extra care was required.

My first tray was a star punch-out. I put on a smile and navigated through the crowd to deliver the tray to a table in the corner. Four men, and I knew Drazen right away. He had red hair cut just below the ears, disheveled in that absolutely precise way. He wore jeans and a grey shirt that showed off his broad shoulders and hard biceps. His full lips stretched across flawless, natural teeth when he saw his tray coming, and I was caught a little off guard by how much I couldn't stop looking at him.

"H-Hi," I stammered. "I'll be your server." I smiled. That always worked. Then I thought happy thoughts because that made my smile genuine, and I watched Drazen move his gaze from my smiling face, over my breasts, to my hips, stopping at my calves. I felt as if I were being applauded again.

He looked back at my face. I stared right back at him, and he pursed his lips. I'd caught him looking, and he seemed justifiably embarrassed.

"Hello," he said. "You're new." His voice resonated like a cello, even over the music.

I checked Yvonne's notes and picked up a short glass with ice and amber liquid from the tray. "You have the Jameson's?"

"Thank you." He nodded to me, keeping his eyes on my face and off my body. Even then, I felt as if I were being eaten alive, sucked to fluid, mouthful by mouthful. A liquid feeling came over me, and I stopped doing my job for half a second while I allowed myself to be completely saturated by that warm feeling. In that moment, of course, someone, a man judging from the weight of impact, pushed or got pushed, and my tray went flying.

For a second, the glasses hung in the air like a handful of glitter, and I thought I could catch them. The sound of the crash lasted too long after three gin and tonics splashed over each guest. I was shocked into silence as everyone at the table stood, hands out, dripping, clothes getting darker at crotches and chests. A collective gasp rose from everyone within splash distance.

Freddie appeared like a zombie smelling fresh brains. "You're fired." He turned to Drazen and said, "Sir, can I get you anything? We have shirts—"

Drazen shook a splash of liquid off his hand. "It's fine."

"I am so sorry," I said.

Freddie got between me and my former boss, as if I would beg him for my job back, which I'd never do, and said, "Get your things."

chapter three.

Fuck it. Fuck that job and everything else. I'd get another one. I promised myself I was going to make it big, and when I did, I would come in here with my freaking entourage and Freddie was going to serve me whatever I wanted for no tip at all. Not even a cent. And Jonathan Drazen was going to sit by me and look at me just like he did before I spilled gin and tonic all over him, but like I'm an equal, not some little piece of candy working for tips.

I slammed my locker shut.

I had to find another job soon. I always paid my housing expenses first, but we owed the studio money, and I couldn't take another dime from Harry.

Freddie strode down the dim hallway, toes pointed out and walking like a duck on a mission.

"Fuck off, Freddie. I'm leaving, and by the way,

you're an—"

"Mister Drazen wants to see you."

"Fuck him. He can't summon me. I don't work for him anymore."

Freddie smiled like a sly cat. "Sometimes he gives the short timers a severance if he feels bad. Nice chunka change. After that, you can get the hell out if you don't want to sleep with him. I'd like to see him not get laid for once."

He took a step closer. I didn't know why he'd get close enough to touch me, so I didn't back away, and when he slapped my ass, I was so stunned I didn't move. He ended the slap with a pinch.

"What did you…?"

But he was already waddling off, elbows bent, as if someone else's life needed to be miserable and he was just the guy to make it so. I stood there with my mouth open, seventy percent mad at him for being a complete molester and thirty percent mad at myself for being too shocked to punch him in the face.

chapter four.

I had pride. I had so much pride that heeling at Jonathan Drazen's beck and call for a "chunka change" was the most humiliating thing I could think of doing. But there I was, in front of his ajar door on the thirtieth floor, knocking, not because I needed the money (which I did), and not because I wanted him to look at me like that again (which I also did), but because I couldn't have been the first waitress ass-slapped, or worse, by Freddie. If Drazen wasn't aware of Freddie's douchebaggery, he needed to be.

The office looked onto the Hollywood Hills, which must have been stunning in daylight. At night, the neighborhood was just a splash of twinkling lights on a black canvas. He stood behind his desk, back to the window, the room's soft lighting a flattering glaze on the perfect skin of his forearms. He wore a fresh pair of jeans and a white shirt. The dark wood and frosted glass accentuated the fact his office was meant to be a comforting space, and even though I knew the setting was manipulating me, I relaxed.

"Come on in," he said.

I stepped onto the carpet, its softness easing the pain caused by my high heels.

"I'm sorry I spilled on you. I'll pay for dry cleaning, if you want."

"I don't want. Sit down." His green eyes flickered in the lamplight. I had to admit he was stunning. His copper hair curled at the edges, and his smile could light a thousand cities. He couldn't have been older than his early thirties.

"I'll stand," I said. I was wearing a short skirt, and judging from the way he'd looked at me on the roof, if I sat down, I'd receive another stare that would make me want to jump him.

"I want to apologize for Freddie," he said. "He's a little more aggressive than he should be."

"We need to talk about that," I said.

He raised an eyebrow and came around to the front of the desk. He wore some cologne that stole the scent of sage leaves on a foggy day: dry, dusty, and clean. He leaned on his desk, putting his hands behind him, and I could see the whole length of his body: broad shoulders, tight waist, and straight hips. He looked at me again, then down to the floor. I felt as if he'd moved his hands off of me, and at once I was thrilled and ashamed. I wasn't going to be intimidated or scared. I wasn't going to let him look away from me. If he wanted to stare, he should stare. I placed my hands on my hips and let my body language challenge him to put his eyes where they wanted to go, not the floor.

Because, fuck him.

"Freddie's a douchebag." I could tell from his expression that was the wrong way to start. I needed to keep opinions and juicy expressions to myself and state facts. "He said you're going to try and sleep with me, for one." He smiled as if he really was going to try to sleep with me and got caught.

"Then," I continued, because I wanted to wipe that smile off his gorgeous face, "he grabbed my ass."

The smile melted as though it was an ice cube in a hot frying pan. He took his hungry eyes off mine, a relief on one hand and a disappointment on the other. "I was going to offer you severance."

"I don't want your money."

"Let me finish."

I nodded, a sting of prickly heat spreading across my cheeks.

"The severance was in case you didn't want to continue working here," he said. "Even though I can't stand the smell of the gin you got on me, I don't think you should lose your job over it. But now that you told me that, what should I do? If I give you severance, it looks like I'm paying you off. And if I unfire you, it looks like I'm letting you stay because I'm afraid of getting sued."

"I get it," I said. "If he said you'd try to sleep with me, then you've got your own shit to hide, and nothing would bring it out better than a lawsuit." I waited a second to see if I could glean anything from his eyes, but he had his business face on, so I put on my sarcasm face.

"Quite a terrible position you're in."

His nod told me he understood me. His position was privileged. He got to make choices about my life based on his convenience. "What do you do, Monica?"

"I'm a waitress."

He smirked, looking at me full on, and I wanted to drop right there. "That's your circumstance. It's not who you are. Law school, maybe?"

"Like hell."

"Teacher, woodworker, volleyball player?" He ran the words together quickly, and I guessed he could come up with another hundred potential professions before he got it right.

"I'm a musician," I said.

"I'd like to see you play sometime."

"I'm not going to sleep with you."

"Indeed." He walked behind his desk. "I assume no one witnessed this alleged ass-grab?"

"Correct."

He opened a drawer and flipped through some files. "I hired Freddie, and he's my responsibility to manage. Your responsibility is to report it to someone besides me." He handed me a slip of paper. It was a standard U.S. Equal Employment Opportunity Commission flyer. "The numbers are on there. File a report. Send me a copy, please. It would protect both of us."

I stared at the paper. Drazen could get into a lot of trouble if enough reports were filed. I intended to tell the authorities what happened because I couldn't stand Freddie, but I felt a little sheepish about getting Drazen cited or investigated.

"You're not an asshole," I said.

He bowed his head, and though I couldn't see his face, I imagined he was smiling. He took a card from his pocket and came back around the desk. "My friend Sam owns the Stock downtown. I think it's a better fit for you. I'll tell him you might call."

When I took the card, I had an urge I couldn't resist. I reached my hand a little farther than I should have and brushed my finger against his. A shot of pleasure drove through me, and his finger flicked to extend the touch.

I had to get away from that guy as fast as possible.

chapter five.

Los Angeles weather in late September was mid-July weather everywhere else—dog's-mouth hot, sweat-through-your-antiperspirant hot, car-exhaust hot. Gabby seemed better than the previous night, but Darren and I were on our toes.

Gabby said she was going for a walk and, trying to make sure she wasn't alone, I suggested she and I get ice cream at the artisanal place on Sunset.

We sat on the outside patio so the noise would mask our conversation. I poked at my strawberry basil ice cream while she considered her wasabi honey longer than she might have a week ago.

"It's good money," she said, trying to talk me into a Thursday night lounge job. "And no pay to play. Just cash and go home."

"I hate those gigs. I hate being background."

"Two hundred dollars? Come on, Monica. You don't have to learn any songs; one rehearsal, maybe two, and we got it."

Gabby had spent her childhood getting her fingers slapped with a ruler every time she made a mistake on the piano. Her playing became so perfect she barely had to work at it. She was so compulsive her every waking moment was spent eating, playing, or thinking about playing, so the word "rehearse" couldn't apply to her because it implied an artist taking time out of their day to get something right, not a compulsive perfectionist basically breathing. She was a genius, and in all likelihood, her genius plus her perfectionist nature drove her depression.

"I only want to sing my own songs," I said.

"You can spin them. Just, come on. If I don't bring a voice on, I'll lose the gig, and I need it." That hitch in her voice meant she was swinging between desperation and emotional flatness, and it terrified me. "Mon, I can't wait for the next Spoken gig. I'm twenty-five, and I don't have a lot of time. *We* don't have a lot of time. Every month goes by, and I'm nobody. God, I don't even have an agent. What will happen to me? I can't take it. I think I'll die if I end up like Frieda DuPree, trying her whole life and then she's in her sixties and still going to band auditions."

"You're not going to end up like Frieda DuPree."

"I have to keep working. Every night that goes by without someone seeing me play is a lost opportunity."

Performance school rote bullshit. Get out and play. Keep working. Play the odds. Teachers told poor kids they might be seen if they busted their violins on the streets if they had to. Dream-feeders. Fuck them. Some of those kids should have gone into accounting, and that line of shit kept them dreaming a few too many years.

I looked at Gabby and her big blue eyes, pleading for consideration. She was mid-anxiety attack. If it continued over the coming weeks, the anxiety attacks would become less frequent and the dead stares into corners more frequent if she didn't take her meds regularly. Then it would be trouble: another suicide attempt, or worse, a success. I loved Gabby. She was like a sister to me, but sometimes I wished for a less burdensome friend.

"Fine," I said. "One time, okay? You can find someone else in all of Los Angeles to do it next time."

Gabby nodded and tapped her thumb and middle finger together. "It's good," she said. "It'll be good, Monica. You'll knock them out. You will." The words had a rote quality, like she said them just to fill space.

"I guess I need it too," I said. "I got fired last night."

"What did you do?"

"Spilled drinks in my boss's lap."

"That Freddie guy?"

"Jonathan Drazen."

"Oh…" She put her hands to her mouth. "He also owns the R.O.Q. Club in Santa Monica. So don't try to work there, either."

"Did you know he's gorgeous?"

A voice came from behind me. "Talking about me again?" Darren had shown up, God bless him.

"Jonathan Drazen fired her last night," Gabby said.

"Who is that?" He sat down, placing his laptop on

the table.

"He didn't do it. Freddie did. Drazen just offered me a severance and referred me to the Stock."

"And apparently he's gorgeous." He raised an eyebrow at me. I shrugged. Darren and I were over each other, but he'd rib me bloody at the slightest sign of weakness. "I haven't heard you talk like that about a guy in a year and a half. I thought maybe you were still in love with me." I must have blushed, or my eyes might have given away some hidden spark of feeling, because Darren snapped open his laptop. "Let's see what kinda wifi I can pick up."

"I don't talk like that about men because I prefer celibacy to bullshit."

Darren tapped away on his laptop. "Jonathan Drazen. Thirty-two. Old man." He looked at me over the screen.

"Do not underestimate how hot he is. I could barely talk."

"Earned his money the old-fashioned way."

"Rich daddy?"

"A long line of them. He makes more in interest than the entire GDP of Burma." Darren scrolled through some web page or another. He loved the internet like most people loved puppies and babies. "Real estate magnate. Our Jonathan the Third..." He drifted off as he scrolled. "BA from Penn. MBA from Stanford. Bazillionaire. He's a real catch if you can tear him away from the four hundred other women he's getting photographed with."

"Lalala. Don't care."

"Why? It's not like you've had sex in...what?"

Darren clicked around, pretending he didn't care about my answer, but I knew he did.

"Men are bad news," I said. "They're a distraction. They make demands."

"Not all men are Kevin."

Kevin was my last boyfriend, the one whose control issues had turned me off to men for eighteen months. "Lalala… not talking about Kevin either." I scraped the bottom of my ice cream cup.

Darren turned his laptop so I could see the screen. "This him?"

Jonathan Drazen stood between a woman and man I didn't recognize. I scrolled through the gossip page. His Irish good looks were undeniable next to anyone, even movie stars.

"He *has* been photographed with an awful lot of women," I said.

"Yeah, he's been a total fuck-around since his divorce, FYI. If you wanted him, he'd probably be game. All I'm saying." He crossed his legs and looked out onto Sunset.

Gabby had a faraway look as she watched the cars. "His wife was Jessica Carnes," Gabby recited as if she was reading a newspaper in her head, "the artist. Drazen married her at her father's place on Venice Beach. She's half-sister to Thomas Deacon, the sports agent at APR, who has a baby with Susan Kincaid, the hostess at the Key Club, whose brother plays basketball with Eugene Testarossa. Our dream agent at WDE."

"One day, Gabster, your obsession with Hollywood interrelationships will pay off." Darren clicked his laptop closed. "But not today."

chapter six.

I think one could be at Hotel K, get blindfolded, taken to the Stock, and believe they'd been driven around and dropped in the same place they started: same pool, same chairs, same couches, same music, and same assholes clutching the same drinks and passing off the same tips. What was different was that there was no Freddie. The Stock had Debbie, a tall Asian lady who wore mandarin collar embroidered shirts and black trousers. She knew every superstar from just their face, and they loved her as much as she loved them. She could tell a movie mogul from an actress and sat them where they'd have the most professional friction. She coordinated the waitresses' tables according to the patron's taste and coddled the girls until they worked like a machine.

She was the nicest person I'd ever worked for.

"Smile, girl," Debbie said. I'd been there a week and

she knew exactly how many tables I could handle, how fast I was compared to the others, and my strong suit, which appeared to be my magnetic personality. "People look at you," she said. "They can't help it. Be smiling."

It was hard to smile. We'd had three good shows in a row, then Vinny disappeared into thin air. We'd banged on his office door in Thai Town, went to his house in East Hollywood, and called four hundred times. No Vinny. Every gig he had lined up for us fell through. My momentum was slowing and I didn't like it.

"What's your freaking problem?" said one dude as he threw a dollar bill and three dimes on my tray. "You need a blast of coke or something?" He'd looked like every other spikey-haired, fake-blonde, Hugo Boss-wearing douchenozzle who namedropped from zero to sixty in three beers. But Debbie had put his name on the ticket, probably as a favor to me. His name was Eugene Testarossa, the one guy at WDE I'd wanted to meet for months. In my depression over stupid Vinny, I hadn't recognized him.

I stalked toward the bathroom on my break and bumped into a hard chest that smelled of sage green and fog.

"Monica," Jonathan said. "Hey. Sam told me he hired you." His green eyes looked down at me and I wanted to break apart under the weight of them. As he looked at me, his face went from amused to concerned. "Are you okay?"

"Fine, just a bad day. Whatever." I stepped toward the bathroom, but he seemed disinclined to let me go so easily.

"I got your report. Thanks. It was very

professional."

"You assumed a waitress couldn't put together a sentence?" His glance down told me I'd been a bitch. He didn't deserve my worst side. I tried to think fast; I didn't want a barrage of questions about my life right then. "The Dodgers lost and I'm from Echo Park and all, so I got a little down."

"The Dodgers won tonight." His pressed lips and bemused eyes told me he understood I was half joking.

I shuffled my feet, feeling like a kid caught lying about kissing behind the gym. "Yeah. Fucking Jesus Renaldo pulling it out in the ninth like that."

"He's got five good pitches in him per game."

"He tends to throw them in the bullpen."

"Or trying to pick a guy off." He shook his head. He looked normal just then, not like the guy behind the desk undressing me with his eyes.

"I'm sorry I was such a bitch just now."

"I'm used to it."

"No, you're not. Come on. People are nice to you all day."

He shrugged. "You lied about why you were upset. I get to lie about how people treat me."

"I'll keep that in mind."

"Yeah," he said, clearing his throat. "I have season tickets on the first base line."

I felt my eyes light up a little, and getting so excited over something someone else had embarrassed me.

"I could bring you sometime," he said.

"You haven't seen a Dodger game until you've seen it from the bleachers. Six dolla seats, yo."

He laughed, and I laughed too. Then Debbie

showed up at the end of the hall.

"Monica!" she called out, tapping her wrist.

"Shit!" I cried out and ran back to my station, turning to give Jonathan a wave before rounding the corner.

I put on a smile and made myself as intensely personable as I could. I saw Jonathan at the head of the bar, talking to Sam and Debbie, laughing at some joke I couldn't hear. When I went to the station to pick up my tray, he looked at me and I felt his sight. He was gorgeous, no doubt. I could write songs about that face, those cheekbones, those eyes, that dry scent.

I wished he'd go away. I tried not to look at him, but he and Sam were still talking at one in the morning. Debbie stood at the end of the service bar, counting receipts, when I came by with a ticket, and I couldn't take it anymore.

"I'm sorry I was talking to Mister Drazen in the hall," I said. "I used to work for him."

"I know."

"How often does he come around here?"

"He and Sam have been close since they went to Stanford together, so... once a week? Should I arrange for him to be here more often?"

My cheeks got hot. To Debbie, who read people like neon street signs, the blushing was visible even in the dim lights. I glanced at him across the bar. He was looking at Debbie and me. He lifted his rocks glass, a bunch of melting ice in the bottom. Sam had gone to take care of some late-night hotel business, and Jonathan was alone.

"Perfect," Debbie said to me. "You will bring him

his refill." She hailed the bartender, a buffed out model who worked his body more than his mind. "Robert, give Mister Drazen's drink to Monica."

"Debbie, really," I said.

"Why?" asked Robert, pouring a glass of single malt from a shelf so high I would have needed a cherry picker to reach it. "I'm not pretty enough?"

"You're plenty pretty," Debbie said. "Now do it." She put her hand on my forearm and spoke quietly. "You need more practice dealing with his social class. For you, as a person. Getting used to it will only benefit you. Now go."

Being mothered was nice, I guess. My mother had been more or less absent since I went to high school, which was about when she and Dad moved to Castaic. I never felt abandoned, but I could have used a hand with the day to day bullshit.

Drazen watched me come around the bar with his scotch. I wondered if he knew that made me uncomfortable or if he even gave it a thought. I wondered if the difference in our relative positions bothered him or turned him on. He was a bazillionaire and a customer. I was a waitress with two nickels making heat. This had to be a turn on.

"Thanks," he said when I placed the napkin and drink on the bar, a job Robert could have done in half the time.

"You're welcome."

We looked at each other for a second or ten. I had nothing to add to the conversation, but his magnetic pull made words irrelevant. I was stepping away to leave when he said, "I meant it, about seeing a game."

"I meant it about the bleachers."

"I like to get to know someone before they drag me out past centerfield." He clinked his ice against the sides of his glass. "The company has to be pretty engaging that far from the plate."

I wanted to mention the stunning color of his eyes. I wanted to touch his hand as it rested on the edges of the bar. Instead I said, "Your fellow fans keep you on your toes, especially if you wear red."

"Can I see you after work?"

The clattering noise in my chest must have been audible. It wasn't that I hadn't been asked out or the object of a proposition in the last year and a half; all of the men who wanted me were simply too easy to politely reject. If I had a brain in my head, I would reject Jonathan Drazen right out of hand. Politely.

"Maybe," I said. "Company's got to be pretty engaging at two thirty in the morning."

Sam showed up, and since I didn't want to be seen talking up my ex-boss, I walked away without confirming that he'd feel engaging at that ungodly hour.

chapter seven.

I spent the next hour and a half talking myself out of meeting with Jonathan after work, if he even showed. He was going to be a distraction, I could tell. I couldn't be in the same room with him without feeling like I needed to touch him.

I thought about Kevin. A fine specimen of a man, he'd had much the same effect on me as Jonathan Drazen, complete with fluttery stomach and tingling cheeks.

I'd been with Darren over six years when he admitted to kissing Dana Fasano. We were in the process of either breaking up or getting married. I went to a party downtown with a friend whose name eluded me right then, and there he was. Kevin was talking to some girl in the corner, and when he glanced over her head, his eyes found mine as if he was looking for them. I froze in place. He had brown eyes and thick black lashes, and when we saw each other, the distance between us became a plucked cello string, vibrating, in a key that sounded like desire.

I didn't see him again for another half an hour, yet I had felt him circling me, tethered, even when we talked to different people. Finally, in the crowded kitchen, he was behind me, and I knew it because I could feel him before I even saw him reach over me to slide a beer from the sink.

"Hi," he said.

"Hi."

He held the beer toward me, his hands slick on the glass, cold water pooling in the crevice between his skin and the bottle. "Is the opener over there?"

I took it from him, overreaching, as I'd done with Drazen, so I could touch his cool, wet hand. Then I put the bottle cap on the metal edge of the counter and pulled down swiftly. The cap bent and popped off, clinking to the floor. I held up the bottle for him. "Here you go."

"Thanks." He considered the drink, then me. "See that girl over there?" He pointed at a girl about my age with short, dark hair and striped leggings.

"Yeah."

"In twenty seconds, she's going to come over here and ask what I'm working on for my show. I don't want to tell her."

"So don't."

As if on cue, the girl saw Kevin and walked over. It was the first time I experienced him as a charmed person, and it would not be the last.

"It would be better if she didn't ask. My paintings are secret before a show. If I tell her, she'll own them. Her soul will own them. I can't explain it." The kitchen was crowded, slowing the striped leggings' progress and pushing us together, forcing us to whisper.

"I get it," I said. I would have gotten anything he said at that point. I would have claimed to understand quantum mechanics if he explained it to me. "They aren't born yet," I continued. "If she sees them while they're being made, she knows them as children. Their insides."

"My God, you get me."

I had no snappy reply. I wanted to get him. I wanted to get everything he said from now on. He touched my chin. "If I kiss you, she'll turn around and go away."

In retrospect, that was the lamest come-on imaginable from him. He'd done much better in the year following. But at the party, the word "kiss" breathed from his beautiful lips, was all I needed. I put my hand on his shoulder, and he slipped one around my waist. Our lips met, and I held back a groan of pleasure. I'd only ever been with Darren, and I loved him. I would always love him, but kissing that man, like that, with his taste of malt and chocolate, uncovered physical sensations I didn't know could come from a kiss. I felt every pore of his tongue, every turn of his lips. The world shut off and my identity became a glow of sexual desire.

I went home barely able to walk from wanting him and completed my breakup with Darren the next day. If desire was supposed to feel like that, I needed more of it. I felt awake, alive, not just sexy, but sexual. Thoughts of him infected me until I saw him again and we tumbled into bed, screwing like wild animals.

When I finally left him, weeping, I realized I'd let my sexuality control and manipulate me through him. He took my music and crushed it under the weight of his own talent. He ignored what I created, dismissing it, degenerating it, so that within three months, I couldn't sing a word and any instrument I picked up became a bludgeon. I'd never felt so creatively dead and so sexually alive.

When I got the strength to walk away from him, I vowed never again.

chapter eight.

I snapped my locker closed, thinking about those Dodger seats on the first base line. A corporation gets a skybox. A real fan gets tickets at field level, luxuries be damned. I'd never seen a game from that angle.

Debbie came into the locker room, buzzing with talk and flirting and locker doors banging, and handed out our tip envelopes. "A good night for everyone," she said, then got close to me. "Someone is waiting for you at the front exit. If you want to avoid him, go through the parking lot, but be nice. He's a friend of the hotel."

"Can I ask you something?"

"Quickly, I have to count out."

"How many drinks did he have?" I asked as quietly as I could.

Debbie smiled as if I'd asked the exact right question. "Two. He nurses like a baby."

"I know you don't know me that well yet, but... would going out the front be a mistake?"

"Only if you take it too seriously."

"Thanks."

Debbie walked off to hand out the rest of the envelopes. What she said had been a relief, actually. It made the boundaries that much clearer. I could hang out, be close to him and feel the buzz of sex between us, but I had to be careful about climbing into bed with him. Fair warning.

chapter nine.

Jonathan Drazen stood in the lobby, talking to Sam, laughing like an old buddy. I wasn't going to approach him with my boss right there. Sam seemed like a fine guy for the fifteen minutes we'd talked. With his white hair and slim build, he looked like a newscaster and had an all-business attitude. I just pushed through the revolving doors, figuring fate had lent a hand in deciding whether or not I'd see Drazen outside a rooftop bar.

I was three steps into the hot night when I heard him call my name.

"You stalking me?" I asked, slowing my steps to the parking lot.

"Just wanted company to walk to my car."

We strolled down Flower Street, the long way to the underground parking lot. Any normal person would have gone through the hotel.

"How do you know Sam?" I asked.

"He introduced me to my ex-wife, which I'm trying not to hold against him."

"You're a good sport," I said. "Have you always been blue?"

He tilted his head a few degrees.

"Dodger fan," I said. "I would've taken you for more of an Angels guy."

"Ah. Because I have money?"

"Kind of."

"I like a little grit," he said, that smile lighting up the night.

"Is that why you met me after work?" I asked, turning toward the parking lot entrance.

"Kind of."

He let me go first into the underground passage, and I felt his eyes on me as I walked. It was not an uncomfortable feeling. When we got to the bottom of the ramp, we stopped. I parked in the employee level and his car was in the valet section. I held up my hand to wave good-bye.

"It was nice to talk to you," I said.

"You too."

We faced each other, walking backward in opposite directions.

"See you around," I said.

"Okay." He waved, tall and beautiful in the flat light and grey parking lot.

"Take care."

"What do I have to say?"

"You have to say please," I said.

"Please."

beg.

"Where do you think you're taking me?"

"Come on. Text a friend and tell them who you're with in case I'm a psycho killer."

chapter ten.

The early hour guaranteed a traffic-free trip to the west side. I'd gotten into his Mercedes convertible thinking most killers don't drive with the top down where everyone could see, so I just let the wind whip my hair into a bird's nest. Jonathan drove with one hand, and as I watched his fingers move and slide on the bottom of the wheel, the hair on the back of it, the strong wrist, I imagined it on me. I grabbed the leather seat, trying to keep my mind on something, anything else, but the leather itself seemed to rub the backs of my thighs the wrong way. "So, you pick up waitresses a lot?"

He smirked and glanced over to me. The wind was doing crazy shit to his hair as well, but it made him look sexy, and I was sure I looked like Medusa. "Only the very attractive ones."

"I guess I should take that as a compliment."

"You definitely should."

"I'm not sleeping with you."

"You mentioned that."

So maybe the rumors were true, and he was a total womanizer. Well, I'd already told him sex was off the table, so he could womanize all he wanted. Didn't matter to me at all. I was driven by curiosity. Who was this guy? What was it like to be him? Not that it mattered, I told myself, because again, I had no time for a heartbreak.

"What's your instrument, Monica? You said you were a musician."

"My voice, mostly," I said. "But I play everything. I play piano, guitar, viola. I learned to play the Theremin last year."

"What is that?"

"Oh, it's beautiful. You actually don't touch it to play it. There's an electrical signal between two antennae, and you move your hands between them to create a sound. It's just the most haunting thing you ever heard."

"You play it without touching it?"

"Yeah, you just move your hands inside it. Like a dance."

"This, I have to see."

When he tipped his head toward me, I thought, oh no. He wants me to play it for him. Never gonna happen. For some reason, the idea of this guy seeing me sing or play made me feel vulnerable, and I wasn't in for that at all. "You can watch people play it on YouTube."

"True. But I want to watch *you* do it."

I didn't know where we were going, so I didn't know how much of a drive we were in for. I wanted to get off the subject of me before I told him something that gave him a hold over me. I had to remember he was my new boss's friend, and I really liked working at the Stock.

"What do you do besides own hotels and pick up very attractive waitresses?"

"I own lots of things, and they all need attention."

He pulled the car to the side of the road. We were on the twistiest part of Mulholland, the part that looked like a desolate park instead of the most expensive real estate in Los Angeles County. A short guardrail stood between the car and a nearly sheer drop down to the valley and its twinkling Saturday night lights.

"Let's go take a look," he said, pulling the emergency brake.

I got out, thankful for the opportunity to uncross my legs, and slammed the door behind me. I walked toward the edge overlooking the city. My heels kept hitting little rocky ditches, but I played it off. They were comfortable, but they weren't hiking boots. I stood close to the guardrail, leaning against it with my knees. I felt him behind me, closing his door and jingling his keys. I'd been to places like that before. There were thousands of them all over the city, which was surrounded by hills and mountains. Way back when, before I'd even kissed Darren, I'd been up to a similar place to squirm around the back of Peter Dunbar's Nissan. And after the prom, I'd come up to drink too much and make love to Darren behind a tree.

"Do you live up here?" I asked.

"I live in Griffith Park." He stepped behind me. "Those bright lights are Universal City. To the right, that black part is the Hollywood reservoir." I could feel his breath on the back of my neck. "Toluca Lake is to the left." He put his hands on my neck, where every nerve ending in my body was now located, following his touch as he stroked me, like the little magnet shavings under plastic I'd played with as a kid. When the pen moved, the shavings moved, and I arched my neck to feel more of him. "The rest," he said, "is hell on Earth. Not recommended."

He kissed me at the base of my neck. His lips were full and soft. His tongue traced a line across my shoulder. I gasped. I had not a single word to say, even when I felt his erection against my back and his hands moved across my stomach, feeling me through my clothes. God, I hadn't been touched like that in so long. When did I decide men were too much trouble? A year and a half since I shed Kevin like a too-warm coat? I couldn't even say. Drazen's lips were more than lips; they were the physical memory of myself before I shut out sex to pursue music.

I twisted, my lips searching for his, my mouth open for him as his was for me. We met there, tongues twisting together, his chest to my back, his hands moving up my shirt, teasing my nipples.

I moaned and turned to face him. He pushed me against the car. The hardness between his legs felt enormous on my thigh. He moved his hand down and pushed my legs open, gripping tight enough to press my jeans against my skin. He looked down at me, and the intensity of the lust in his eyes was nearly intimidating, but I was way past sense. Miles. The thought of saying, "No, stop, I need sleep so I'm fresh for rehearsals tomorrow," didn't even occur to me. He pushed his hips between my legs and kissed me again. I was hungry for him. A white hot ball of heat grew beneath my hips. We kept kissing and grinding, hands everywhere. I pinched his nipple through his shirt and he gasped, biting my neck. I hated my clothes. I hated every layer of fabric between myself and his cock. I wanted to feel skin sweating above mine, his dick rigid and hot, his hands at my breasts. I wanted those hard, dry thrusts to be real, slick, sliding inside me.

The siren blast split my ears. I almost choked on my own spit. Jonathan looked over at the police car and the tension in his neck was the last thing I saw before the light got too bright to see anything. I lowered my legs, and when he got off me, he held his hand out to help me off the hood.

"Good morning," came a male voice from behind the driver's side light. The passenger door opened, and a female cop got out.

"Good morning," Jonathan and I answered like two kids greeting their third grade teacher. He wove his fingers in mine. The female cop shone her flashlight in my face. I flinched.

"You okay, miss?"

"Yeah."

"Can you step away from the gentleman, please? Come toward me."

I did, hands out so she knew I wasn't reaching for anything. The cop pulled me out of earshot.

"Do you know this guy?" she asked, shining a little light into my pupils to see if I was on anything stronger than pheromones.

"Yes."

"Are you here of your own free will?"

"Yes."

"That was pretty hot." She snapped her little light down. "Next time, get a room, okay?"

chapter eleven.

Things cooled on the way home. I kept my legs crossed and his hand stayed on the gear shifter. When I told Jonathan the lady cop said we should get a room, he laughed.

"If only she knew who she was talking about," he said. After a few seconds, he stopped at a light and turned to me. "So, what's up with you saying you're not sleeping with me, then pushing up against my dick on the hood of my car?"

I was a little annoyed with the question, because he brought me there and he started kissing my neck, but I also couldn't pretend I wasn't just as responsible for the raw heat of the scene.

"I just..." I had to pause and think. The light changed, and when he turned his head back to the road, I felt like I could talk. "I have things I'm doing. I can't be up all night fucking because my voice gets messed up. I can't think about a man, any man, nothing personal, when I should be writing songs. Carving out enough nights for song writing, between gigs and working, is hard enough without making time for a boyfriend. So, I mean, I had to give up something in life, and it's men."

He nodded and thought about it. He rubbed his chin, which had a little bit of stubble. My neck remembered it very fondly. "I get it."

"So, I'm sorry I led you on. That was careless."

His laugh was loud and inappropriate, considering what I'd just said, but he didn't seem embarrassed.

"What's so funny?" I asked.

"You're taking all my best lines."

"Didn't mean to steal your thunder."

"No problem. I enjoyed hearing it."

I leaned back and watched the scenery change from the twisted forestation of Mulholland to the expanse of the 101. How did I end up in this car, at four in the morning, with a known womanizer? Yes, he was gorgeous and warm and knew all the right places and ways to touch me, but really? How stupid would I be? How many women had fallen for this crap, and I was going to be another one in line?

The wind made it hard to talk until he pulled off downtown. "What's with you and sleeping around?" I asked.

"What do you mean?"

"All the women. You have a reputation."

"Do I?" He smirked, not looking at me as he drove. "And that didn't chase you away?"

"I trust myself. I trust my instincts and my resolve.

You just make me curious is all."

He shrugged. "What do you think your reputation is?"

"I don't have one."

"Of course you do. Everyone does. When people talk about Monica, what do they say, besides that she's beautiful?"

I let the compliment slide. Coming from someone who had almost made his way into my pants, it didn't mean much. "I guess they say I'm ambitious. I hope they say I'm talented. My friend Darren would say I'm cold."

"Did he try to get you into bed, too?"

"Shut up." He glanced at me and we smiled at each other. "I was with him for six and a half years, so it's not like he had to try for a long time."

"Was it a hard breakup?" He stopped at a light and turned his gaze to me, ready to offer me sympathy or words of wisdom.

"No. It was the easiest thing we ever did." I couldn't discern what he was thinking from the way he looked at me, but he got serious, draining his tone of all flirtation.

"Easy for *you?*"

"Both. It was dying for a long time."

He looked out his window, rubbing his lips with two fingertips.

"You want to say something you're not saying," I said. "I don't want to be your girlfriend, so being honest isn't going to come back and bite you on the ass."

The Stock, and my car, were a block away. He pulled up to the curb. He put the Mercedes in park but didn't turn the key.

"You really want to know?"

"Yeah."

"Why?"

"Because you make me curious."

He smirked. "My wife and I were married that long. It wasn't easy." He rubbed the steering wheel, and I realized he regretted answering even the first part of the question. It was too late for me to give up on him now, so I waited until he said, "She left and took everything with her."

"I don't understand. Are you broke?"

He put the car into drive and turned to me. "She didn't take a dime. She took everything that *mattered.*"

I felt sorry and then I felt stupid for feeling any kind of sympathy. I wanted to hold his hand and tell him he'd get over it someday, but nothing could have been less appropriate.

"I'm kinda hungry," I said. "There's this food truck thing on First and Olive. In a parking lot? You can come if you want."

"It's four in the morning."

"Don't come. Your call."

"You're a tough customer. Anyone ever tell you that?"

I shrugged. I really was hungry, and nothing sounded better than a little Kogi kimchi right then.

chapter twelve.

Jonathan was right in mentioning the time. Four in the morning was pretty late, as evidenced by the fact that he found a place for the car half a block away. We walked into the lot, against the traffic of twenty- and thirty-something partiers as they filtered out, one third more sober than they had been when they got there, carrying food folded in wax paper or swishing around eco-friendly containers. The lot was smallish, being in the middle of downtown and not in front of a Costco. The only parked vehicles lined the chain link fence, brightly painted trucks spewing luscious smells from all over the globe. My Kogi truck was there, as well as a gourmet popcorn truck, artisanal grilled cheese, lobster poppers, ice cream, sushi, and Mongolian barbecue. The night's litter dotted the asphalt, hard white from the brash floodlights brought by the truck owners. The truck stops were informal and gathered by tweet and rumor. Each truck brought their own tables and chairs, garbage pail, and lights. The customers came between midnight and whenever.

I scanned the lot for someone I knew, hoping I'd find someone to say hello to on one hand and wishing Jonathan and I could stay alone on the other.

"My Kogi truck is over there," I said.

"I'm going to Korea next week. The last think I need is to fill up on Kogi. Have you had the Tipo's Tacos?"

"Tacos? Really?"

"Come on." He took my hand and pulled me over to the taco truck. "You're not a vegetarian or anything?"

"No."

"*Hola*," he said to the guy in the window, who looked to be about my age or younger with a wide smile and little moustache. "*Que tal?*" he continued. That was about the extent of my Spanish, but not Jonathan's. He started rattling off stuff, asking questions, and if the laughter between him and the guy with the little moustache was any indication, *joking* fluidly. If I'd closed my eyes, I'd have thought he was a different person.

"You speak Spanish?" I asked.

"I live in Los Angeles," Jonathan replied as if his answer was the most obvious in the world.

"You don't speak it?" Little Moustache asked me.

"No."

He said something to Jonathan, and there was more conversation, which made me feel left out. They were obviously talking about me.

"He wants to know if you're as smart as you are

beautiful," Jonathan said.

"What did you tell him?"

"Prospects are good, but I need time to get to know you better."

"Anywhere in that conversation, did you order me a *pastor?*"

"Just one?"

"Yes. Just one."

"They're small." He made a circle with his hands, smiling like an old grandma talking to her granddaughter about being too damn skinny.

I pinched his side, and there wasn't much to grab. It was hard and tight. "One," I said, trying to forget that I'd touched him.

We sat at a long table. A few trucks were breaking down for the night. There was a feeling of quiet and finality, the feeling he and I had outlasted the late nighters and deep partiers. I finished my taco in three bites and turned around, putting my back to the table and stretching my legs.

He took a swig of his water and touched my bicep with his thumb. "No tattoos?"

"No. Why?"

"I don't know. Mid-twenties. Musician. Lives in Echo Park. You need tattoos and piercings to get into that club."

I shook my head. "I went a few times, but couldn't commit to anything. My best friend Gabby has a few. I went with her once, and I couldn't decide what to get. And anyway, it would have been awkward."

"Why?" He was working on his last taco, so I guess I felt like I should do the talking until he finished.

"She was getting something important. On the inside of her wrist, she got the words *Never Again* on the scars she made when she cut herself. I couldn't diminish it by getting some stupid thing on me."

He ate his last bite and balled up his napkin. "What happened that made her try to commit suicide?"

"We have no idea. She doesn't even know. Just life." I wanted to tell him I'd found her, and been with her in the hospital, and that I took care of her, but I thought I'd gotten heavy enough. "I have a piercing, though," I said. "Wanna see?"

"I can see your ears from here."

I lifted my shirt to show him my navel ring with its little fake diamond. "Yes, it hurt."

"Ah," he said. "Lovely."

He touched it, then spread his fingers over my stomach. His pinkie grazed the top of my waistband, and I took in a deep gasp. He put a little pressure toward him on my waist, and I followed it, kissing him deeply. His stubble scratched my lips and his tongue tasted of the water he'd just drunk. I put my hands on his cheeks, weaving my fingers in his hair.

It was sweet, and doomed, and pointless, but it was late, and he was handsome and funny. I may not have been interested in having a boyfriend, but I wasn't made of stone.

When Little Moustache had to break down the table, we had to admit it was time to go. The sky had gone from navy to cyan, and the air warmed with the appearance of the first arc of the sun.

We got to his car before he had to feed the meter. We didn't say anything as he pulled into the parking lot at the Stock and went down two stories to my lonely Honda, sitting in the employee section. I opened the door with a clack that echoed in the empty underground lot.

"Thanks," he said. "I'll probably see you at the hotel sometime."

"We can pretend this never happened."

"Up to you." He touched my cheek with his fingertips, and I felt like an electrical cable to my nervous system went live. "I wouldn't mind finishing the job."

"Let's not promise each other anything."

"All right. No promises," he said.

"No lies," I replied.

"See you around."

We parted without a good-bye kiss.

chapter thirteen.

Gabby and I lived in the house I grew up in, which was on the second steepest hill in Los Angeles. When my parents moved, they let me live in the house for rent that equaled the property taxes plus utilities. I was sure I'd never need to move. I had two bedrooms and a little yard. The house had been a worthless piece of crap in a bad neighborhood when they bought it in the 1980s. Now it had a cardiologist to the west of it and a converted Montessori school that cost $1,800 a month to the east.

The night Jonathan Drazen took me up to Mulholland Drive, I returned to find Darren sleeping on my couch. We had agreed to not leave Gabby alone until we knew she was okay, and she'd gotten no better after a week on her meds. The first blue light of morning came through the drapes, so I could see well enough to step around the pizza box he'd left on the floor and get into the bathroom.

I looked at myself in the mirror. The convertible had wreaked havoc with my hair and my makeup was gone, probably all over Jonathan Drazen's face.

I still felt his touch: his lips on my neck, his hands feeling my breasts through my shirt. My fingers traced where his had been, and my pussy felt like an overripe fruit. I stuck my hand in my jeans, one knee on the toilet bowl, and came so fast and hard under the ugly fluorescent lights that my back arched and I moaned at my own touch. It was a waste of time. I wanted him as much after I came as I did before.

My God, I thought, how did I do this to myself? What have I become?

I needed to never see him again. I didn't need his lips or his firm hands. If I needed to take care of my body's needs, I could find a man easily enough. I didn't need one so pissed at his ex-wife he'd make me fall in love with him before apologizing for leading me on. He wanted to hurt women, and nothing froze my creative juices like heartache. No, I decided as I went back out to the kitchen, anyone but Jonathan.

Darren was already making coffee.

"Where were you?" he asked. "It's six thirty already."

"Driving all over the west side with I-won't-say."

"Mister Gorgeous?" He said it without jealousy or teasing.

"Yep."

"He's nice to you?"

"He wants to sleep with me, so it's hard to say if

he's being nice or being manipulative," I said. "How's Gabby?"

"Same." He got out two cups and a near-dead carton of half-and-half. "She's volatile, then deadened. She started shaking because she wasn't playing last night. Missed opportunity and all that. Then she rocked back and forth for half an hour."

"Did you sit her at the piano?"

"Yeah, that worked. We need something to happen for her."

"She'll still be who she is," I said. "She could play the Staples Center, and she'd be this way."

"But she could afford to get care, the right meds, maybe therapy. Something." I nodded. He was right. They were stymied by poverty. "And Vinny? I haven't heard a damn thing from that guy. I tried calling him and his mailbox is full." He was losing his shit, standing there with a coffee cup in his hand.

"We have six more months on our contract with him and we're out," I said.

"She doesn't have six months, Mon."

"Okay, I get it." I held him by the biceps and looked him in the face.

"She's like she was the last time, when you found her. I don't want—"

"Darren! Stop!"

But it was too late. The stress of the evening had gotten to him. He blinked hard and tears dripped down his cheeks. I put my arms around him, and we held each other in the middle of the kitchen until the coffeemaker beeped. He wiped his eyes with his sleeve, still holding the empty cup. "I'm working the music store this morning. Will you stay with her until rehearsal?"

"Yeah."

"Can I shower here? My water heater's busted."

"Knock yourself out. Just hang the towel."

He strode out of the kitchen, and I was left there with our dripping sink and filthy floor. The roof leaked, and the foundation was cracked from the last earthquake swarm. It had been nice to sit in that Mercedes and drive around with someone who never spent a minute agonizing about money. It had been nice to not worry about anything but physical pleasure and what to do with it for a couple of hours. Real nice.

Darren's laptop was on the kitchen table, set to some Pro Tools thing he probably hadn't gotten a chance to touch in the middle of taking care of Gabby. I fixed my coffee and slid into the chair, opening the internet browser. We stole bandwidth from the Montessori school during off hours, so I checked my email. I remembered my conversation with Jonathan about his ex-wife, so I did a search for her: Jessica Carnes.

I got a different set of pictures than Darren had shown us the other day. Jessica was an abstract and conceptual artist. Searching under Google Images brought back a treasury of pictures of the artist and her art, which despite Kevin schooling me in the vocabulary of the visual arts, I didn't get at all.

Jessica had long blond hair and an Ivory Girl complexion. She might have worn a stitch of makeup and maybe used hot rollers. She wore nice flats, but flats nonetheless. Her skirts were long and her demeanor was modest. She was my exact opposite. I had long brown hair and black eyes. I wore makeup, tight jeans, short skirts, and the highest heels I could manage. And black. I wore a lot of black, a color I hadn't given a thought to until I saw Jessica in every cream, ecru, and pastel on the palette.

On page three, I came across a wedding photo. I clicked through.

The page had been built by her agent, and it showed a beachside extravaganza the likes of which I could only aspire to waitress. I scrolled down, looking for his face. I found him here and there with people I didn't know or side-by-side with his bride. A picture at the bottom stopped me. I sighed as if the air had been forced out of my lungs by an outside force. Jessica and Jonathan stood together, separated from the crowds. Her back was three-quarters to the camera, and he faced her. He was speaking, his eyes joyous, happy, his face an open book about love. He looked like a different man with his fingertips resting on Jessica's collarbone. I knew exactly how that touch felt, and I envied that collarbone enough to snap the laptop closed.

chapter fourteen.

I tapped my foot. Studio time was bought by the hour and not cheap, yet Gabby and I were the only ones there. She was at the piano, of course, running her fingers over the keys with her usual brilliance, but it was only therapy, not real practice. Darren's drums took twenty minutes to set up. The chitchat and apologies would take another fifteen minutes, and I still had to practice some dumb standards for the solo gig at Frontage that night.

I sat on a wooden bench facing the glass separating the studio from the control room. The room stank of cigarettes and human funk. The soundproofing on the walls and ceiling was foam, porous by necessity, and thus holding cells for germs and odor. Though I thought I'd rubbed away the ache Jonathan had caused, I woke up with it, and a good scrub and an arched back in the shower did nothing to dispel the feel of him. I needed to get to work. Letting this guy under my skin was counterproductive already.

I whispered, "I've got you, under my skin." Then I sang the first verse.

It was a good song. It was missing how I really felt: frustrated and angry. So I belted out the last line of the chorus, *I've got you, under my skin,* without Sinatra's little snappy croon, but a longing, accusatory howl.

"Hang on," Gabby said. She took a second to find the melody, and I sang the chorus the way I wanted it played.

"Wow, that's not how Sinatra did it," she said.

"Play it loungey, like we're seducing someone." I tapped her a slower rhythm, and she caught onto it. "Right, Gabs. That's it."

I stood up and took the rest of the song, owning it, singing as if the intrusion was unacceptable, as if insects crawled inside me, because I didn't want anyone under my skin. I wanted to be left alone to do my work.

Having the guys here to record it so I could hear it would have been nice, but I could tell I was onto something. The back room at Frontage was small, so I needed less rage and more discomfort. More sadness. More disappointment in myself for letting it happen, and begging the pain away. If I could nail that, I might actually enjoy singing a few standards at a restaurant. Or I might get fired for changing them. No way to know.

I did it again, from the top. The first time I sang the word, "skin," I felt Jonathan's hands on me and didn't resist the pleasure and warmth. I sang right through it, and when Gabby accompanied, she put her own sadness into it. I felt it. It was my song now.

My phone rang: Darren.

"Where the hell are you?"

"Harry just called me. His mother is sick in Arizona. He's out. For good."

I would have said something like, *so no bassist, no band,* but Gabby would have heard, and she wasn't ready for any kind of upset.

"And you're not here because?"

He sighed. "I got held up at work. I'll be there in twenty. Tomorrow night, I have a favor to ask."

"Yeah?"

"I have a date. Can you get her home after your gig and make sure she takes her meds?"

"Yeah."

"Thanks, Mon."

"Go get laid."

I clicked the phone off and used the rest of the time to work on our performance.

chapter fifteen.

Thursday afternoon shift at the Stock was slow by Saturday night standards. I earned less money, but the atmosphere was more relaxed. There was always a minute to chill with Debbie at the service bar. I liked her more and more all the time. I tried to keep it light and hold my energy up. Just because this gig tonight wasn't my own songwriting, I still wanted to do a good job. But after Darren's call and the sputtering dissolution of the band, I lost the mojo, and I just sounded like Sinatra on barbiturates. I had no idea how to get that heat back.

Debbie got off her phone as I slid table ten's ticket across the bar. Robert snapped it up and poured my rounds.

"I think he likes you," Debbie said, indicating Robert. He was hot in his black T-shirt and Celtic tattoos.

"Not my type."

"What is your type?"

I shrugged. "Nonexistent."

"Okay, well, finish with this table and go on your break. Could you go down to Sam's office and make a copy of next week's schedule?" She handed me a slip of paper with the calendar. The waitstaff hung around waiting for it every week as our station placement and hours determined not only how much money we'd make over the next seven days, but our social and family plans as well. And here she was giving it to me two hours early. She smiled and patted my arm before walking off to greet three men in suits.

I went to the bathroom and freshened up, then headed for Sam's office.

It wasn't a warm, fabulously decorated place like Jonathan's at K. It was totally utilitarian, with a linoleum floor and metal filing cabinets. The copy machine was in there, and I put the schedule on the glass without turning the lights on. The windows gave enough afternoon light.

The energy saver was on, meaning the copier was ice cold. I tapped start and waited. Lord knew how long it would take. I stretched my neck and hummed, then whispered the lyrics to *Under My Skin*.

I gasped when I smelled his dry scent. When I turned, Jonathan stood in the doorway with his arms crossed. That was the first time I'd seen him in daylight, and the sunlight made him look more human, more substantial, more present, and more gorgeous, if that was even possible.

"Jonathan."

"Hi."

I realized the deal with the schedule copying just then. "Debbie sent me up here."

"You didn't know she was a yenta?"

"You're very persistent."

"I just kept telling myself I didn't want you, but we said no lies, and I think that includes lying to myself. How about you?"

I didn't know what to say. I had shut out thoughts of him for almost a week. I thought about baseball, chord progressions, and getting a new manager whenever he came into my mind. So having him in front of me was like opening a closet door and having all the stuff come tumbling out.

I took a step forward, and he did, too. We were in each other's arms in a second, mouths attached, tongues twisting. He reached back and closed the door.

Okay, I was going to get this over with now. Me and him. Right there. Just get it done so I could move on. He thrust me onto the desk and I opened my legs, wrapping them around his waist. He was pushing against me again, like on the hood of the Mercedes, a million years ago.

He put his hands up my shirt, across my stomach and to my breasts.

"Yes?" he gasped.

"Yes," I whispered. "Yes to everything."

"Yes," he whispered in my ear, then pushed my bra up and cupped my tits, finding my nipples and rubbing them with his thumbs. My hips levitated from the desk, and I made some noise deep in my throat. Damn, he was good. Lots of practice. He knew exactly what to do.

He looked down at my chest, nipples hardening from his touch and the cool air. "My God, Monica, you are magnificent."

I laughed, because being admired like that made me nervous, but he shut me up when he put his mouth on one nipple and his fingers on the other, pressing and twisting. My legs tightened around him, hitching my skirt up to my waist. With only my panties between me and his jeans, he felt harder and more forceful. He pushed against me, and I flowed with him, my hips to his rhythm as I gripped his hair. I'd almost come like that, eons ago, with some guy in freshman year I couldn't even remember now, and it felt like it might happen again.

As if reading my mind, he pulled away. His own breathing was heavy as he looked at me, not as if he was undressing me with his eyes, but as if he was making plans for the body in front of him. He moved his hands down my sides and pulled my skirt up, bunching it at the waist. My underwear bottoms, which I hadn't given a thought to when I'd dressed in the morning, were the only thing between me and the world.

"Listen," I started, "I don't know if Sam would think this is ok."

He put his fingertips to my mouth, and I shushed. Let him explain to Sam. Let me get fired. I parted my lips and took two of his fingers in my mouth, sucking them down to the back.

"Ah, Monica," was all he said as he pulled them out, slowly, and pushed them back in at the same pace. I cupped my tongue around them and sucked. Not too hard, just enough. I knew I was doing it right when his eyelids closed just a little, and he opened his mouth for something between a gasp and an *aah*. He rubbed them over my bottom lip, curling it back, then put them back in my mouth. I took them eagerly, tasting his skin, feeling his warm breath on my face.

He slid his fingers out and stepped back, taking his crotch away from mine. I suddenly felt exposed and started to close my legs, but he pressed them apart. I reached for his buckle, but he pulled away.

"I want to touch you," I said.

"Not yet."

"I'm going crazy."

"No, you're not. Not enough."

With that, he moved the crotch of my panties to the side and put the finger he'd just removed from my mouth onto my wet folds. We both gasped. Then he slid two fingers into me. Slowly.

"Oh, God," I whispered.

He slipped them out without a word and put his thumb on the thin strip of cotton covering my clit. Lightly. Barely touching it. Just enough so I knew it was there, and he leaned over to kiss me, flicking his tongue in time with his thumbnail as it gently scratched the fabric of my underwear.

I thrust my hips forward. His fingers went deep into me, but the thumb wouldn't press down any harder. It just grazed the cotton as he glided his two fingers in and out.

"What do you want?" he asked.

"I want you to fuck me."

"What's the magic word?"

"Now?"

His fingers worked my body while he bent down to whisper into my ear. "You have three minutes of break left."

"I don't care."

"I'm going to spend hours fucking you."

My hips pushed against his hand, but he kept control: a light touch of the thumb and a slow grind with the fingers. I was on fire. I thought I had known what that meant, but I didn't.

"After your shift."

"I have a gig right after. We have to do it now." He might have considered it for the next three thrusts, but he didn't give my clit more than a stroke through fabric. I couldn't decide if that was pleasure or torture.

"After your gig," he said. "I have a dinner meeting anyway. Meet me at the hotel tonight. Room 3423."

"I have to take care of my roommate."

"Figure it out."

He pulled his fingers out of me. I felt the loss of them and his tormenting thumb so deeply I moaned. Sitting there, splayed and nearly naked on Sam's desk, I felt foolish and exposed, not to mention ravenously aroused.

"Don't." I didn't have anything more to say, except don't stop there; don't leave me like this. My eyes must have pleaded with him for some release, because his face, with its parted lips and heavy lids, shone with a lustful satisfaction. He knew I wanted him to fuck me for hours, starting on that desk. "You are despicable," I said.

He pulled my skirt down, and when he leaned down to kiss me, I returned it with no little anger on my lips. "Too true. And tonight, you're mine."

"What if I don't show?"

"You'll show."

beg.

After opening the door as little as possible, as if to protect my destroyed modesty, he was gone.

chapter sixteen.

I had another three hours to work, and I couldn't keep my mind on the task at hand: pouring drinks. A moron could do it. First example: Robert. A hunk by any measure, but dumb as a post.

He slid the tray over the service bar. Each had the requisite alcohol as listed on the order ticket, clockwise from twelve o'clock, where he'd put the ticket. My job was to fill each glass with mixers from the soda gun and juice bin.

Like I said, a moron could do it. But I stood there, with Debbie next to me checking stuff off the inventory list, and I put soda in a whiskey. I stared at the glass and watched it over flow and why? Because the pain between my legs was uncomfortable and exquisite, and I was counting down the hours before I could get home and release it.

"Whoa!" Robert shouted, waking me up. "You got soda all over the tray!"

"I'm sorry!"

"Monica," Debbie said, slipping her pen onto the top of the clipboard, "come sit with me."

She pulled me over to an empty table by the kitchen door. We tried to keep it clear until the bar got too packed. I pressed my legs together when I sat even though my skirt was long enough. I felt like she could see my arousal.

Debbie placed her clipboard in front of her and leaned forward. "What's happening? You took the wrong order to Frazier Upton; you stepped on Jennifer Roberg's foot. That's not how we do service here."

"Why did you do that, Debbie? Why did you set me up to meet Jonathan upstairs?"

"I saw you looking at him the other night. I thought it would be a nice surprise."

"If you could avoid doing that again, that would be great."

"Of course. I'm sorry, I thought I was doing you a favor."

"You were. It's just…" I looked at my hands in my lap. "He's… I don't know." I felt suddenly embarrassed talking about a man's hold over me with my manager. I should have been mad at her, but in the world I lived in, she had done me a kindness, and it wasn't like he'd raped me. I'd loved it. I hated it ending when it did. "I just don't need to be with anyone right now. Or ever. I had this boyfriend, Kevin, a year and a little ago. He wouldn't let me sing. It was awful, but what I'm trying to say is, I don't want to be that person again."

"Okay." Debbie sat up straight. She pushed her long, straight hair out of her face with a single, French-manicured finger and got down to business. "I am going to tell you things you need to hear, but don't want to. Are you okay with that?"

"Sure."

"Jonathan Drazen is not going to stay with you long enough to care what you do with your spare time. He is very attracted to you, that much I can see. But he is in love with one woman, and one woman only."

"His ex-wife."

Debbie nodded. "When Jessica left, he begged her to stay. She wouldn't. He broke down at a shareholder meeting. It was ugly. He was humiliated. He's *still* humiliated. He won't put himself in that position again, I promise you. So if you like him, I suggest you enjoy yourself with him. He will treat you very well, and then you'll go your separate ways. He can be a valuable friend."

I nodded. I got it. I felt comforted, in a way, that I could meet him later, have mattress-bending sex, then go home without worrying. I knew I wasn't getting involved, and if he had the same idea, I was safe.

Debbie gathered her things and started to stand, but I wasn't done.

"Why did she leave?" I asked.

"Another man," she said, "and everyone knew it."

"Ouch."

Debbie nodded. "Ouch is right. It should never happen to any of us."

chapter seventeen.

I hated gigs like Frontage. I had to sing songs someone else wrote to people who weren't there to see me. I had to sing through waiters taking orders and customers being seated. I couldn't sing too loud or I'd disturb everyone, and I couldn't improvise at all. Ever. I was background.

But it was money, if not a lot, and it was practice. It wasn't as if Vinny had shown up and booked anything fabulous. It wasn't as if he'd shown up at all in the past two weeks. I simply had nothing else going on.

We had a dressing room with a smudged mirror and filth on everything. Sometime in the eighties, a tube of lipstick had been jammed into the seam between the two pieces of plywood that made up the counter, and the red goo that was out of reach of a folded paper towel had turned brown and crusty. The carpet stank of beer vomit, and the bathroom had been casually wiped down a few days previous. I felt like a superstar.

Gabby was already out there, tinkling the piano. She had a jazzy way of rolling her fingers across the keys, creating a melody from nothing, building on it, and landing into something else without a hitch. Her bag was open on the counter, and I did what Darren and I always did. I took out her meds and made sure she had one less Marplan than she had last night. Ten milligrams, twice a day. Eleven pills in the bottle. Darren had texted me this morning with the number twelve. Good.

I called him. He was headed out for another date with this girl whose name he wouldn't reveal.

"Hey, Mon," he said.

"Eleven," I said.

"Thanks."

"What are you doing tonight?" I asked.

"Date."

"Are you going to tell me her name?" I sat on the torn pleather chair, letting my short skirt ride up since I was alone. My hair was up, and red lipstick coated my lips like lacquer. I looked like a 1950s pinup.

"Not yet," he said.

"Is it an early date or a late date?" I swallowed hard. I was about to ask a lot.

"Maybe both. Why?"

"I wanted to…" I drifted off, because I wanted to meet Jonathan and relieve the ache he created, but I didn't want to get into too much detail with Darren.

"Ask. I'm shaving and it's messing up the phone."

"I wanted to see Jonathan Drazen tonight. After the gig. Right after. I can be home to watch Gabby by eleven."

"Can't. Her boss got her tickets to *Madame Bovary*."

Great. A date including a musical would go from dinner at seven p.m. to curtains at eleven thirty. He must like this girl.

"Sorry," he said. I heard the water running.

"No problem." I hung up.

Eight months before I ever worked at K, I found Gabby sitting at the kitchen sink, on the high stool I'd used to get cereal as a kid. Her head was on the counter and one wrist had flopped over, spilling blood onto the floor.

I'm so sorry I messed up the floor, Monica, she'd said the next day, in her hospital bed. That was what she was worried about: That I would be mad I had to clean up the floor. I'd just ripped up the whole thing and put in new press-on vinyl tiles. I couldn't find another way to think about something besides how dead and cold she looked when I pulled her off the stool, or the blood trapped in the drain catch, or the way I'd screamed at her the day before for eating graham crackers in the living room, or the way she'd wept when Darren and I broke up, eons ago. I cried over cracking linoleum flooring because the ambulance had arrived a full nine and a half minutes after I called, and I spent them slapping her because it made her groan and I didn't know what else to do to prove she was alive.

So though I wanted Jonathan to treat me like his own personal toy for a few hours, I had to get Gabby home and stay there until the next morning, when Darren would show up.

The lights kept me from seeing any of the diners. I

smiled at a bunch of silhouettes because even though I couldn't see them, they could see me.

Gabrielle hit the first song, *Someone to Watch Over Me,* then went to *Stormy Weather.* I had my groove on then. I sang with the feeling she and I had practiced, but as I got to the middle of *Cheek to Cheek,* I caught a whiff of cologne I recognized: Jonathan's. Someone was wearing his cologne, and the weight between my legs came back from the memory of the afternoon. I sang about his cheek on mine, about the scent and feel of him. *Under My Skin* came out like a seduction. I sang the words, but all I could feel was sex, the need for it. I begged for it with the lyrics, the snappy little Sinatra tune gone, replaced by a moan for gratification.

When my voice fell off the last note, I was ready for that hotel room.

They applauded, quiet but earnest. You weren't supposed to clap at all at these types of gigs, and I said, "Thank you" with an embarrassed smile. I was convinced they could see my arousal like a dark patch soaking through my dress. I looked back at Gabby, and she gave me a thumbs up. I think I must have been a hundred shades of blush. I put the mike down and the spotlights went out. The diners started up their conversations again, and I headed back to the shitty dressing room.

Jonathan was in a booth, staring at me.

Of course that was where the cologne smell had come from. The source. It wasn't like he'd gotten it at Barney's. If it wasn't a handmade scent, I'd eat my shoe. But I hadn't even thought of that until I saw him in a booth at Frontage with a gorgeous redhead sipping a cosmopolitan. He tipped his glass to me.

He leaned toward the redhead and whispered something to her. Right into her ear. Like tipping his glass to me and breathing on her in any ten second interval was perfectly okay.

I was going to run and get as far from him as possible. I couldn't believe what I'd almost done. I wasn't kidding myself into thinking monogamy was on the table, but I'd think a day would pass before he'd put his hand up someone else's skirt, or that he'd take the trouble to not shove it right in my face.

But instead of running away like a sensible person, I walked up to the booth. "Hi, Jonathan."

"Monica," he said. "This is Teresa."

I nodded and smiled, and she held her glass up to me. "That was beautiful."

"Thanks."

"You were incredible," Jonathan said. "I've never heard anything like that." I stared at him. Something had changed in his face. I couldn't pin it down. Softer? Was he tired? Or did Teresa have a relaxing effect on him? His happiness made me feel evil and sharp.

"I've never heard of a man trying to sandwich another woman between fingering me and fucking me in the same day."

Teresa, who looked as though she was one hundred percent lady, almost spit out a mouthful of her cosmopolitan. Jonathan laughed too. I personally didn't find any of this funny. I stepped back, and Theresa stood as well. Maybe she was pissed. Maybe her laugh was the nervous kind or maybe I'd just shocked her. But she was as composed as possible as she turned to Jonathan and said, "I'm going to the ladies'."

He nodded, then scooted over once she was gone. "Would you like to sit?"

"No."

"For someone who doesn't want to get involved, you have a way of being involved."

"Even I have limits."

"She's a natural redhead." His look was full deadpan, and though what he said had a hundred filthy connotations, the one non-pornographic one became apparent with the straight-faced look.

"She's your sister," I said.

"Two years between us. She'd appreciate it if you assumed I was older."

"I'm so embarrassed," I said. "I have to apologize to her."

"Are you going to sit? Or am I just going to stare at your body without touching you?"

I slid in next to him, and he put his arm around me, his fingertips brushing my neck.

"What are you doing here?" I asked.

"I was having dinner with my sister. No, I was not stalking you, though I have to say again, I think you have a gift. I think I felt a half a tear, right here." He touched the inside corner of his eye.

"Are you making fun of me?"

"No. I promise you. You were... I don't have a word big enough." He looked at my face, and I noticed his eyelashes were copper, like his hair. I was overcome by his presence. "Now I know what you're protecting by not getting entangled."

"Thank you," I said. "I appreciate that. I really do."

He ran his finger over my collarbone with just enough pressure to make me breathe a little more deeply. "Am I seeing you tonight?"

I tried to stay cool, but I wanted him all over again. "I don't think I can. I'm not avoiding you. I have something else going on. Tomorrow?"

He shrugged. He must have thought I was playing games with him, which he'd probably be exquisitely sensitive about after the cheating wife. But I wasn't playing a game. Not at all.

"I have a flight out at five tomorrow. After two weeks, you might forget me."

"I should do to you what you did to me this afternoon," I said.

He let out a short snort of a laugh into his whiskey. "You don't have the self-control."

"What?"

"You heard me."

"You're wrong."

"Wanna bet?"

"Yeah. I wanna bet."

He pulled me close and spoke so softly I could barely hear him. "You get me to beg for it, and tomorrow I will take you to Tiffany on Rodeo Drive where you can pick out anything you want."

"Anything?"

"Anything."

"And what if I don't? Which I won't, but just for argument's sake."

"Then you cancel whatever it is you're doing, and I take you back to my house, where you will obey my every command until the sun comes up."

"I am not scrubbing your kitchen floor."

He smirked. "That's not what I had in mind."

I hadn't noticed the piano had stopped until I mentioned the kitchen floor.

"I'll be right back," I said, getting out of the booth before I had a chance to explain that I wasn't ditching him or manipulating him. I'd let Gabby go off by herself, and I didn't know if she'd seen me with him and taken a cab home.

I ran into Teresa in the hall on the way to the dressing room.

"I am so sorry," I said. "I was rude and unbecoming."

"My brother's an asshole, so I don't blame you." She said it with a smile, taking my hand and squeezing. "We both loved your voice."

"Thank you. I have to go. I'll try to see you on the way out."

I got into the dressing room just as Gabby shouldered her bag.

"I was looking for you," she said.

"I was talking to Jonathan. You ready to go? I want to see him on the way out."

"He's here? Oh my God, Mon, he can help us get an agent or something. Another manager. Anything."

"He's not in the business, Gabs, please come on."

She tugged my sleeve. "Wait. First of all, everyone's in the business, even if they're not. Okay? And what are you hiding from me? What?" She was a few inches shorter and looked up at me like she could pierce me with her eyes.

"Nothing."

"Monica."

"I want to go home." I took a step toward the door, but Gabby leaned against it. I dropped my bag, giving in. "Fine, he wants to make this bet, and it has to do with sex, and I'm not hanging out with him tonight, I'm hanging out with you."

"Cancel with me."

"No."

"Why not?"

"Because Darren would kill me."

"God damn the two of you!" she shouted.

"Gabs, please. Give me a break."

"No, you guys won't leave me alone to take a dump and you think I'm too stupid to notice? Now you have the chance to get the ear of a major fucking player—"

"He's not—"

"Shut up. Because you don't know anything. He teaches business at UCLA where Janet Terova heads up the Industry Relations board, and you know who that is, right?"

I sighed. I felt like I was taking a quiz.

"Arnie Sanderson's ex-wife?"

"Eugene Testarossa's boss. Right. Him."

"Gabby, if something happened because I went to have sex with some guy I barely even know…"

She put her hands on my arms and looked up at me with those big stinking blue eyes, the ones that had rolled to the back of her head and could only be brought back with a slap in the face, and said, "I promise I will not try to kill myself tonight."

"Your word is the last thing I should believe."

"I tried to kill myself because I felt hopeless. You do

this, I have hope. Okay?"

"You're whoring me out."

"Am I taking a cab home or not?"

I had to admit, the temptation was painful, almost physically so. Here she was, not only giving me permission to leave her alone and promising not to hurt herself, but pushing me out the door.

The exquisite ache between my legs grew to a distracting level when I thought about being with Jonathan. The afternoon's frustration had turned into a longing that seemed bigger than my body.

Right then Darren's face showed up in my mind. He looked disappointed and angry.

I pushed past Gabby and went out to Jonathan and Teresa, who had moved to the bar. He put his hand on the back of my neck when I got close enough, and I whispered in his ear, "If I win, you cancel your flight and see me tomorrow night."

"And no Tiffany?" he asked, smirking.

"Yes, Tiffany. If you win, I'm at your command until sunrise. And after the sun comes up, I'll scrub your floors." He laughed. I didn't know exactly what he was laughing at, unless it was the presumption that he didn't already have a team of people to sterilize his house, but I smiled back at him because it was a stupid offer and I knew it.

Gabby situated herself at the end of the bar and ordered something. I hoped it was soda. Alcohol's a depressant, and she could assure me she had hope all she wanted. I didn't believe she had as much control as she asserted.

"You drive a hard bargain." He put his drink down.

"And you're funny. I never know what's going to come out of your mouth next."

I had a million jokes about what was going in my mouth, but I kept them to myself as I pulled him into the back room.

chapter eighteen.

The dressing room was locked. I was momentarily stumped, but I remembered there was another one for men. I took his hand and led him deeper into the back, passing the kitchen and backmost hallway, to the least populated part of the club.

"I'm really liking this scrubbing idea," he said as I pulled him into the second dressing room, which was as gross as the first, and slammed the door behind me. If he had more wisecracks, they got swallowed in a kiss. I ran my fingers through his hair, pressing his face to mine, then ran them down the length of his body. I pushed him onto the chair, which squeaked when he fell into it.

I kneeled in front of him, the industrial carpet digging into my knees, and opened his fly. I stroked the hardness under his boxers until I teased out his cock. It was rock hard and gorgeous.

"You ready?" I asked.

"You are really cute."

He held his arms out as if to say *come at me*.

I pulled up his shirt and kissed his stomach, which was hard and tight, down the line of hair, until I got to his base. I put him between my lips, kissed it, sucking the length on one side, then the other, running my tongue up and down the taut skin, tasting the sharpness of it. He took a deep breath. I flattened my tongue against the underside and ran it up to the end, then put the head in my mouth, sucking it on the way out. I tasted a salty drop of moisture on his tip.

I looked up at him as I slid it into my mouth again. His lips parted and he looked straight at me, moving my hair from my eyes. Perfect. I moved down, sliding the whole huge length of him into my open mouth.

"Oh," he whispered as I took him to the bottom. I moved my head up and down, taking all of him with every stroke, sucking on the way out, rubbing him with my tongue on the way in. I looked up at him again, going slow, letting him see every inch of his dick going in my mouth. I picked up the pace slightly, then gave three really fast strokes. He sighed and thrust his hips forward, jamming himself down my throat. I had him. All I had to do was slow down and tease him so close he'd beg me to finish him.

But he put his head back and looked at the ceiling, groaning deep in his throat. It was such a position of surrender, I couldn't do it. I couldn't stop. I was going to make him come way before he begged.

beg.

He was going to have me at his beck and call until sunrise.

I didn't like jewelry that much anyway.

chapter nineteen.

He'd smirked when he'd given me his address and tried to give me directions, but I knew where he lived, give or take. He was up in the park, where the lawyers and magnates play. I remembered Debbie's edict to just have fun, but the fact I'd failed in my mission to get him to take me to Tiffany rankled. Not that I really had anything to go with the carats I would have made him buy me, but failure wasn't something I took lightly, especially if it meant I'd been weak.

The valet pulled up with his dark green Jaguar. "Can I drive you to your car?" Jonathan asked.

"I'm in the lot," I said. "It's fine."

He put his face close to mine, until I could feel his breath in my ear. "If you don't want to go home with me, I won't hold you to it. We can wait, or we can call it off."

"A bet's a bet."

He brushed his nose on my cheek. "You sure? I can be demanding."

"So can I."

He stepped back and smiled. "Not tonight, you're not." He moved onto the curb. "I'll leave the gate open for you." He got into the car and drove off. I watched it head down La Brea, swaggering just like he did.

When I went inside, Gabby had already called a cab. I could smell a vodka tonic on her breath, but she seemed relatively sober.

"Are you sure you're going to be all right?" I said.

"Monica, you want to go, so just go. I'm tired of being babied."

And that was that. I put her in a cab and walked to my car.

My phone buzzed as I got into my little Honda. It was Vinny. Fucking Vinny.

"Where are you?" I asked.

"Vegas, baby." He was somewhere loud and unruly, yelling into the phone.

"We've been looking for you. The band broke up."

"I can't hear you. Listen, Sexybitch, you did a gig tonight at that shithole on Santa Monica?"

"Fron—"

"Eugene Testarossa's partner was there. Testarossa himself wants to see you. So you text me when you're up next, and I'll call him back and he'll show up. Bang! You're in."

"Vinny, I can't—"

"Text me, baby. Love you."

He cut the call.

What an asshole. He goes to Vegas for how long and now he wants his fifteen percent because I got my own gig? Oh no. That wasn't going to work. I texted him,

—*You're fired*—

I was at my car when the phone dinged.

—*Fuck I am. You signed a contract*—

—*The band signed a contract. The band didn't play tonight. I played solo*—

There was a longer pause, and I sat in the driver's seat waiting to hear back, my night of subservience forgotten.

—*Good luck getting WDE to take your call*—

I shut off my phone. I wanted to throw it, but I couldn't afford to replace it when I smashed it into a million pieces. He was right. No one at WDE was going to take a call or email from me. They'd contacted Vinny. I wouldn't get past the first round of assistants. Their job was to filter out artists. I could sing *Under My Skin* a hundred more times and never get another opportunity like this.

I think I looked out the window for fifteen minutes, resigning myself to the fact that I had a manager I hated and distrusted, and he was going to take a chunk of money from me from now until I accepted my Grammy.

I started the engine, but I had forgotten where I was going. Then that weight between my legs came back. Shit. I had an evening of wild sex planned with a rich womanizer who liked cute broke chicks. I was worrying about Vinny Landfillian. Fuck him. I hated Los Angeles.

All money and connections.

He can be a valuable friend.

All I needed was a lawyer to unravel that contract, and I was about to screw a guy who must have had a hundred sharky lawyers on speed dial. All I had to do was let him boss me around all night. The pleasure would be all mine.

I put the car in drive and headed east to Griffith Park.

It was wrong. My mother didn't raise me like that. She raised a nice girl who cared about her body more than her career. I didn't know who that girl was or what she wanted out of life though. I knew who I was. And the only thing I wanted more than Jonathan Drazen's body was an agent at WDE.

chapter twenty.

The houses north of Los Feliz Boulevard aren't dream houses. A dream house in Los Angeles has four walls and a roof and maybe heat, but no one can afford it. The houses up in Griffith Park are scenery. They're owned by other people, the people who live on the other side. Not nouveau riche rock stars and actors. Old money. Generations' worth of trust funds. Three thousand square feet was a palace behind ten-foot hedges. I drove up the winding pass. Never having looked at the addresses before, I was at a loss to find them. It was as if you were supposed to just *know* where you were going because you belonged there.

I finally found the address under a gigantic fig tree with a brass plaque next to it, announcing the tree's status as a protected landmark. The gate opened for me, and I went up the drive and parked next to the Jag.

I sat in the car and looked at the house, convincing myself I still had a choice between going in or going home. The house was a craftsman, all warm lighting and dark woods. The porch was as big as my living room, leading to a wide, thick door. It was closed.

I took a deep breath.

Bottom line: He was hot, he was charming, and he didn't want anything out of me but the same thing I wanted. Unless he wanted me to clean his bathroom. I took hours to clean a bathroom, and I wasn't cleaning his.

I slid my phone out of my purse and called Darren.

"Hi," I said. "How was the show?"

"Fantastic. What's up?"

"I thought you should know…" I swallowed hard. "I sent Gabby home in a cab."

"You what?"

"She's tired of being followed around."

"And where are you?" He was pissed. He sounded like he was in the middle of a street, with people everywhere.

"Griffith Park. I can explain more later."

"No, explain now why you let a suicidal woman go home alone when her meds obviously aren't working and she's showing the same behaviors she did just before you found her bleeding into your kitchen sink."

"She's fine."

"This is completely irresponsible."

He hung up, which was a huge favor. I didn't want to tell him *why* I'd ditched Gabby.

I got out and walked up to the porch. Stained glass windows bordered the door. The light on the other side was soft and inviting. *This would be all right. Just fine.*

I knocked so softly, he couldn't have heard me unless he'd been waiting. I needed to see if he'd found something else to occupy him or if he was looking forward to seeing me. That could set the timbre for what I could request in the way of a warm call to WDE on my behalf.

The door opened immediately.

He wore the same button down shirt and jeans he'd worn at Frontage. His feet were bare, and in his right hand, he held a glass containing whiskey on ice.

I stood with my bag in front of me, which didn't stop him from looking at me as if he wanted to eat me alive. He leaned on the door jamb and swirled his drink. "I thought you weren't coming. I was starting to think I was losing my touch."

"This is a nice house."

"I wanted to mention something about that, before you come in." He paused, and I waited. Despite the distractions of the past half hour, I was back to wanting to put my tongue all over his body. "All bets are on?" he asked.

"I'm yours to command."

He took my bag and put it on a side table. "Turn around."

I put my back to him. My car sat in the drive, next to his, the gate to the street wide open. He clicked the button on a little handheld box, and the gate slid closed.

The ice in his glass clinked, and I felt the touch of his hand at the base of my neck, then a tug as he unzipped my dress. "Jonathan…"

"No one can see."

The zipper went down past my lower back, and he slowly pulled it open. The sleeves slipped off a little when his hand, cold from the drink, touched between my shoulder blades. He ran his hand up to my neck, then over my right shoulder, pushing the dress off. Then he ran his hand to the left shoulder, until the dress slipped off and pooled around my ankles. I felt a breeze over my body. He slipped his finger under the bra strap. "Take this off."

I did, dropping it to the porch floor. He stroked under my waistband. He wanted that off too. I knew it, and I complied. I was fully naked except for my shoes, with my back to him.

"Face me."

I did. I'd never felt so naked in my life as he took his time looking me over.

"Hands behind your back."

I think if anyone else had gotten to command number four, I would have started laughing, but he wasn't anyone else.

"You doing okay?" he asked, stepping up to me. He put the glass to my lips and tipped it. Warmth filled my chest. It was good whiskey. The single malt I'd suspected.

"It's warm tonight," I said.

He put his face up to mine and whispered, "Infield fly rule. What is it?"

He kissed my neck as I answered. "When there's a force play at third, any fly hit inside the baselines, whether it's caught or not, means the batter's automatically out."

"Why?" He bit the corner of my neck and shoulder,

and I gasped.

"To prevent an intentional error that would manufacture a double play."

"You are very real." He enunciated each word.

He drank the last of the whiskey and took an ice cube in his teeth. He put his face to mine and pressed the ice cube to my lips. I sucked on it, then took it from him, holding it in my mouth.

He took half a step back. I must have been a sight: naked but for my heels, hands behind my back, with an ice cube in my mouth. "And you are stunning," he said, lifting his glass. He put the cold base of it to my nipple, and I groaned as it hardened. He touched the other one, chilling it to a rock.

He bent down and warmed my breast with his mouth, sucking on the hard tip, pulling on it with lip-blunted teeth. I gasped, but couldn't open my mouth farther or I'd lose the ice. I guess that wouldn't have been the worst tragedy, but I knew the game was to keep the ice in my teeth. His attention to my breast made me groan, awakening the warmth in my crotch. The ice in my mouth melted, dripping down my chin and neck, tingling a wet path to my stomach. He licked the droplets that found their way to my breasts, warming cooled skin with his tongue. When I thought I couldn't take another minute of his attention without falling down from the pleasure of it, he stood straight and put his mouth over mine, sucking the ice back.

He crunched it and said, "Come on in."

I stepped past the threshold, and he closed the door behind me. The living room was impeccable in dark woods and Persian carpets. The bookcases were full. The whole place was the exact opposite of the cold modernity of his hotels.

Jonathan stood in front of me, watching my eyes take in the details of his house. The paintings. The stained glass. The clean corners and fluffed pillows. He kissed me again and, having forgotten the edict about the position of my hands, I put my arms around him. His hands warmed my back, his touch solid and strong. He kissed my cheek and neck. "Go upstairs. There's a room with the light on and an open door. Sit on the end of the bed. I'm going to lock up down here."

"Okay," I said because I needed to hear the sound of my own voice at the end of so many commands. I backed up, and he watched me as I turned and went up the stairs.

The room he wanted was right in front of me. There were other doors, all closed. I heard him banging around downstairs with locks and lights. I could peek in one room, just to see, then say I was looking for the bathroom, but the idea lasted the time it took for me to step into the room with the single, glowing lamp.

I sat at the edge of the bed. It must have been a guest bedroom. There were no pictures, no personal effects, just a hardwood bed and matching craftsman style dressers.

He seemed to take forever, and just as I was about to get up and see if he was all right, I heard him coming, one slow step at a time, up the stairs.

He was still dressed and had a bottle of water. He held it out to me.

"I'm good. Thanks."

"You look uncomfortable."

"You took a long time."

He kneeled in front of me and touched my knee. "I'm sorry, Monica. Can you forgive me?"

Before I could answer, he kissed inside my knee. "I think so," I said. "If you keep doing that."

He looked up at me, all green eyes and messy red hair. He moved his lips up my thigh, spreading my legs. A tingle went up the inside of my thighs as he ran his hands up them, the edge of his watch made a light scratch on sensitive skin. He picked my leg up, and I fell back as he lightly kissed the outside of my mound.

"Ah, Jonathan," I whispered, stroking his hair. He spread my legs farther, kissing between them. He slipped his finger into my wetness, and I gasped and remember the afternoon and Sam's desk. This time was different. When I looked down at him, his eyes were closed with intensity as he flicked his tongue over my clit. I think I said his name again. He flicked again. He was so light with it. Like he didn't want me to come.

As if he read my mind, he stood up, undressing so quickly I had only a second to admire his body, with its light hair and perfect angles. He flipped a condom out of his pocket and got it on without missing a beat, then lodged himself on top of me, his dick like a rock and everywhere it should be except inside me. We kissed. He tasted perfectly of whiskey and desire. I wanted him. I wanted every inch of him. He was right outside, pressing in, the head of his cock a tingle at my opening. I twisted my hips to move him in, but he backed off, picking his head up to look at me.

"Please," I said.

"Not yet."

He slid his dick up my cleft without entering me, rubbing the length of him on my clit, sending waves of pleasure through me. I was so wet, he slid back and forth. I spread my legs as far as I could and moved with him. I could come like this, but I didn't want to. I wanted him inside me. This would feel like masturbation compared to his cock being where it belonged.

"Please," I said again.

"Not yet."

"Jesus, Jonathan. What do you want?" My sex ached for him. It didn't feel empty. It felt full to bursting, a throbbing, pounding hunger filling my skin.

"I want you to want it," he said.

"I do. My God, I do."

In response, he pushed harder, increasing the pressure without entering me. "No, you don't. Not enough."

I knew what he wanted, and I was willing to give it to him. "Please. I'm begging you. I'm begging. I'll do anything you want. I'll be anything you want. Just don't—"

He drove his dick into me with a ferocity that shocked me and turned the last word into a cry. He stopped for a second, as if he'd been shaken by the violence of his initial thrust.

"Don't stop," I gasped. "Don't make me beg again."

He buried his face in my neck and fucked me, pushing inside, pressing his body against my clit, his cock rubbing with each stroke, until I couldn't take it anymore, and then he stopped.

"What?" I groaned.

"You want to come?"

"Yes. Fuck. Yes."

"Beg for it."

"Fuck you." I pushed his chest. I was on fire, so close to orgasm, nearly unable to think complete thoughts. He pushed himself in me once, then stopped. It was a burst of sensation between my legs, then nothing. I looked up at him. He was enjoying himself, and he could keep going as long as he needed to.

"Please. Fuck you."

"Close." He stroked again, a taste of what I could have. He went slowly, too slowly, moving enough to keep me hot, but not enough to get me off. I put a hand between my legs and he grabbed both my wrists, holding them against the mattress with all his weight, rocking his hips back and forth just a little.

I had never felt anything like that. It wasn't an orgasm, because I had not an ounce of release, only the firing nerve endings and blasting heat between my legs. I was sweating everywhere. Tendrils of hair clung to my face, but his hands held mine down,.

"I want to come," I groaned.

"I want you to come."

"Let me. Please." I said it so softly I didn't even think he'd hear me. "Please. Please. *Please…*" With every *please*, I got more desperate and more quiet. On the last plea, he pulled out of me and pushed back in, all the way, and then again, until everything went hot red. I said his name over and over, going limp everywhere, and still the orgasm went on and on. His mouth was at my ear, and I could hear his groan as I finally stopped coming. His arms wrapped around me, tightening as he came, a guttural *ahh* rattling his throat with each slowing thrust.

"Holy fuck," he whispered into my neck.

"Thank you," I said. "Thank you."

He propped himself up on his elbows and kissed my face from my chin, to my right cheek, to my forehead, and back down my left cheek, and to my chin again. His eyes flicked to his watch.

"Sun rises at 5:38 a.m. You're mine for four more hours."

"I don't think I can take four more hours of that."

"Don't sell yourself short." He rolled off me, and we just stared at the ceiling, letting our breathing get back to normal.

I had never experienced anything like that, not with Kevin and certainly not with Darren. I didn't know I could sit on the brink for that long or just how many brinks there were. I didn't know I could give someone else control over what I felt.

It felt as though, after that orgasm, I should have to sleep for hours, or I wouldn't want sex for at least a month, but neither was the case. I was energized, and I wanted it again.

"Where are you flying off to tomorrow?" I asked.

"Korea. I'm putting a hotel up in Seoul."

"Can I ask you a question?"

"Uh oh."

"Your house. You have all the original everything in here, and the hotels are, like, white and chrome."

"This house was built for a family a hundred years ago. It was a home. People want to feel like they're *away* from home when they go to a hotel."

"Right. That makes sense."

"I thought you were going to bail on me."

"I got held up talking to my manager. Ex-manager. Jerk-off." I tucked my head on his shoulder and ran my fingertips up and down his chest. I couldn't keep my hands off him.

"This the guy who disappeared?"

I propped myself up on my elbows and kissed his shoulder and down his chest. I could still smell some of the dusty cologne past the sheen of sweat built up from our sex. "This guy from WDE was at Frontage and called him. He wants his boss to see me. But I fired Vinny, and now he won't give me the contact."

"Why'd you fire him?"

"Because he's an asshole. I'll find a way to get Testarossa to take my call myself." I worked my way down his stomach, over his hip bones, with my lips and tongue. I was aroused all over again. He put his hands on my shoulders.

"WDE? That's Arnie Sanderson, right?"

Arnie Sanderson owned WDE and was the single most inaccessible person in the world. Even his own clients had to make appointments to get a call, and regular schlub WDE clients, who were some of the top paid people in entertainment, never met the guy.

"Arnie Sanderson. Yeah," I said. Jonathan's dick was hard again already.

"I'll call him for you."

"I'm not about to suck your dick so you'll make a call for me."

"And I'm not making the call so you'll suck my dick. So, now that we've cleared that up, can you get on with it?"

I looked up at him. He smiled from ear to ear and

put one hand under his head. I licked his dick's length with the flattest part of my tongue. When I got to the top, I slid the entire length of it down my throat.

He breathed a deep *ahh* and said, "Where did you learn to do that?"

"Los Angeles High School of Performing Arts," I said. "They taught me how to open my throat to sing. Then Kevin Wainwright taught me how to put his dick down it."

He laughed. "I'd like to thank LA Unified and Kevin Whatever for this moment."

I couldn't help but grin, which kept me from engaging in the task at hand. "I like you, Jonathan."

"Feeling's mutual, Monica."

chapter twenty-one.

We collapsed from exhaustion around five thirty a.m. Two hours later, I woke up with a sore cunt and a dry throat. Jonathan's arm was draped over me. His breath came in heavy, slow rhythms. I looked at him sleeping, closely inspecting him for the first time. His copper-colored lashes fluttered under soft brows. Faded freckles dotted his nose. He was truly beautiful, and seeing him with those eyes, I realized I could easily fall for this man. I was walking on a precipice even letting myself stare at him for this long.

I slipped out from under his arm and went to find my clothes.

My dress and underwear were draped over a chair by the door and smelled like last night's whiskey and fresh porch air. I slipped into them and went into the kitchen for water.

I looked onto the backyard, with its dark green furniture and bean-shaped pool, sipping my water. I ran over the night in my mind, which was hard, because after a certain point, it just became a blur of skin, sweat, and orgasms. I must have said his name a hundred times, starting with me begging him to fuck me and ending with an orgasm he'd delayed eternally. When he finally let me come, it must have lasted fifteen minutes.

The first time he had thrust into me with such force, it was almost like he wanted to shut me up. Like he was saying, "here, take it, but please stop."

Please. I'm begging you. I'm begging. I'll do anything you want. I'll be anything you want. Just don't—

I was going to stay *don't stop*, but in a different circumstance, when the love of your life was walking out the door, you might say *don't leave.*

The buzz of a phone brought me back to my senses. I was making stuff up. The phone buzzed again. I didn't know if it was mine, but I located the source on the kitchen counter, plugged into the wall. Jonathan's phone, and it was facing up.

The caller: *Jess.*

Ex-wife.

Fuck.

I threw the rest of the water down my throat and put the glass in the sink. I had to go. I didn't want to get in the middle of whatever that was.

"Good morning," he said, sleep all over his face, T-shirt stretched over his perfect body.

"I took the glass from the rack and got water from the little thing in the fridge door. Didn't even open it." He shrugged, and I relaxed. He didn't seem to feel invaded.

"Can I make you coffee?" he asked. "I can scramble eggs if you want."

"No, I'm okay."

As I rinsed the glass, he came up behind me and kissed my neck, fingering my zipper. "How about another go?"

"The sun is up," I teased. I wanted another go. On the counter. On the floor. His lips caressed my earlobe, and I leaned my head back.

He slipped the dress's zipper down. "You need to beg again. You're good at it." He kissed my back. I wanted to. I wanted to cry for it, one more time, before he became a memory. He pushed my dress off my shoulders with a perfect touch that rode between firm and light, a touch on a collarbone, maybe, like the one caught on camera from his wedding day.

"Your phone rang," I said. Stupid. Another go would have been nice, but it was too late now.

"It's always ringing." He reached inside the dress and caressed my breasts, nipples hardening at his touch.

The phone buzzed. His lips left me, and I knew he was looking at it. His hands fell, and a palpable chill filled the room. I cleared my throat.

"I think I need to take this," he said, zipping me back up.

"Sure," I whispered. "My shoes are upstairs."

I walked to the door, and when I looked back, he was popping the cable from the phone. His hands could have been shaking. I couldn't tell.

I scooped up my shoes from the bedroom floor and went back to the kitchen. He was on the patio, elbows on his knees, looking at the flagstones with the phone pressed to his ear. His hands gestured, but I couldn't hear him. It wasn't my business.

"Good-bye, Jonathan," I said before I slipped out the front door.

To be continued...

This series is complete. The reading order is below.

The entire series is structured like a serial TV show. Novellas were released every four to six weeks, with a break between sequences. Each novella episode was between 20 and 50 thousand words, and ended with unanswered questions.

Sequence 1
Beg
Tease
Submit

Sequence 2
Control
Burn
Resist

Sequence 3
Sing

Supplemental, optional reads—

Jessica/Sharon (ebook only - to be read after *Submit*)
Rachel (ebook only - to be read after *Burn*)
Monica (ebook only - to be read after *Sing*)

I have a Facebook fan page run by me, for official news and announcements, and a Facebook group which is run by my fans. Check them out.

Email me at *cdreiss.writer@gmail.com*

My website is cdreiss.com.

I'm on Pinterest, Tumblr, Twitter and Instagram with varying degrees of frequency.

And, of course, if you have any feelings about this book you'd like to share, kindly leave a review.

Printed in Great Britain
by Amazon.co.uk, Ltd.,
Marston Gate.